This edition first published in 2020 by Gecko Press
PO Box 9335, Wellington 6141, New Zealand
info@geckopress.com

Original title: Mijn Mama

Distributed in the United States and Canada by Lerner Publishing Group, lernerbooks.com
Distributed in the United Kingdom by Bounce Sales and Marketing, bouncemarketing.co.uk
Distributed in Australia and New Zealand by Walker Books Australia, walkerbooks.com.au

This publication has been made possible with financial support from the Dutch Foundation for Literature.

Nederlands letterenfonds
dutch foundation
for literature

Edited by Penelope Todd
Typesetting by Esther Chua
Printed in China by Everbest Printing Co. Ltd, an accredited ISO 14001 & FSC-certified printer

ISBN hardback: 9781776572670
ISBN paperback: 9781776572687

Annemarie van Haeringen

Translated by Bill Nagelkerke

GECKO PRESS

I’ve known my mama for a long time.
For my whole life, actually.

Mama enjoys playing with me and my cars.
I like that, as long as she tidies them up afterwards.
They have to be neatly parked in my toy box.

"VROOM, VROOM!"

My mama always looks nice
Sometimes she puts on lipstick.
Then I want a little bit too, and that's okay.
And sometimes I try to make Mama's dress prettier, but that's not okay.

Mama and I always do the shopping together.

“Rice, vegetables, fruit…have I forgotten anything?”

I’m very good at carrying things.

I’m even better at tidying things up. A bag of chips is gone in no time!

When the weather's good, we go on the swings.
Who can go the highest?
Of course I help Mama a bit, otherwise she'd never win…

"HIGHER!"

I love climbing mountains.
I scramble up as quick as I can, high above the clouds.
When I reach the top, Mama gives me a kiss.

Actually, I'm always the one in charge.

"CLIPPITY-CLOP, CLIPPITY-CLOP!
MAMA GALLOP! MAMA TROT!"

I’m good at hiding.

No one can find me, not even my mama.

…and then suddenly I shout:

“PEEKABOO!”

That scares her to death! I laugh and laugh.

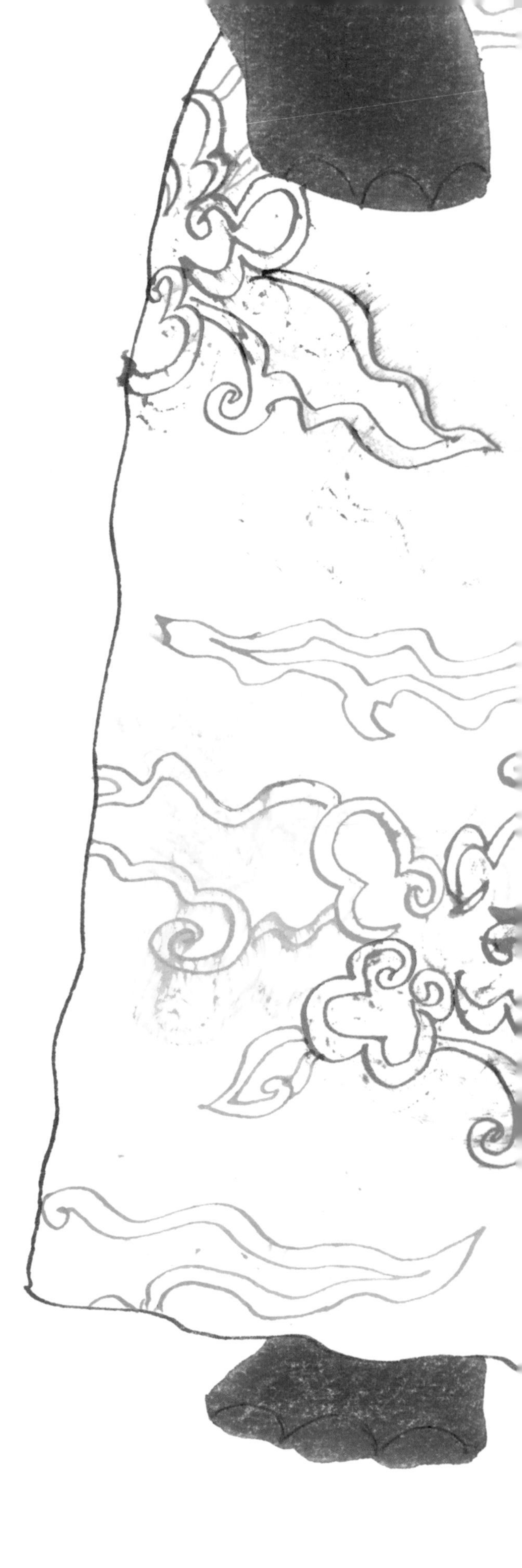

I like watering the plants.
The funny thing is that when I do,
it always starts to rain.

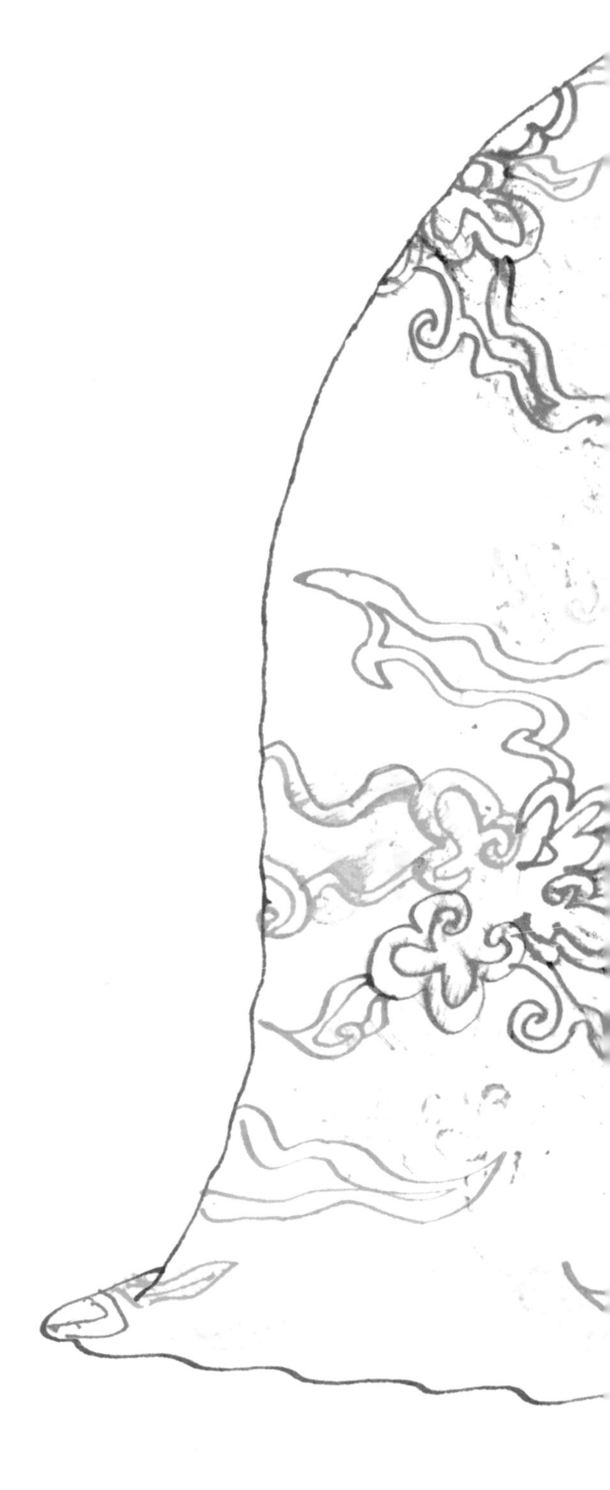

My mama is never angry with me...
But when she is, she's really ANGRY!
Then she explains why...
and that takes a very long time.

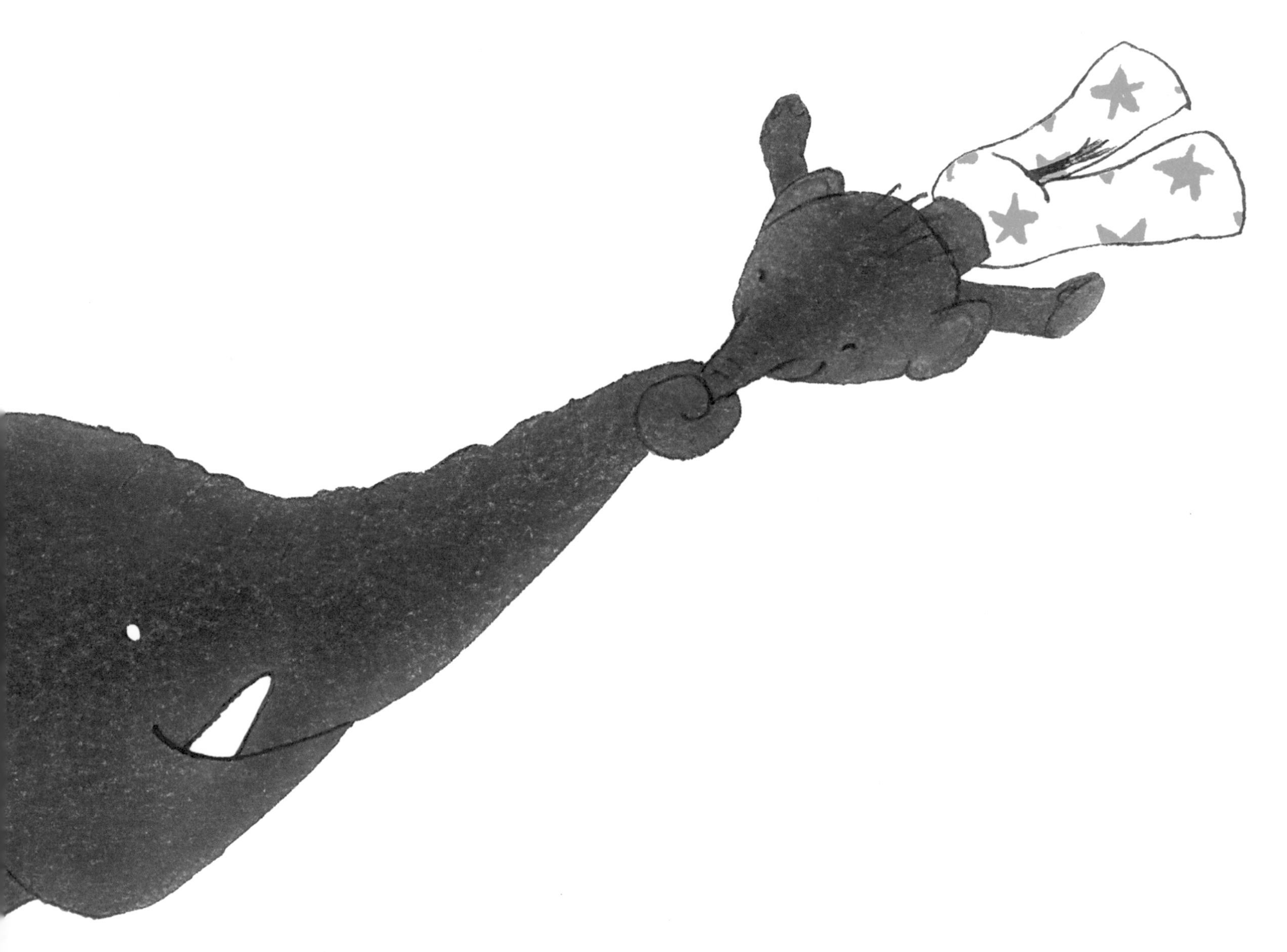

I really want to fly.

Mama says that you can do anything if you really want to.

It's true. You can see I'm already good at it.

But my mama finds it hard to let me go.

At bedtime, my mama shakes the stars off my pants.

I give her a big hug and say:

“Goodnight, stars, see you tomorrow!”